W9-AIE-538

The Third Gift

LINDA SUE PARK

Illustrated by
BAGRAM IBATOULLINE

CLARION BOOKS
HOUGHTON MIFFLIN HARCOURT
BOSTON | NEW YORK | 2011

I would like to thank the Reverend Mindy Adams,
the Reverend Galen H. Meyer, and the Reverend Dr. John B. Paterson
for reviewing the manuscript of this story. Any errors are my own.

CLARION BOOKS
215 Park Avenue South, New York, New York 10003

Clarion Books is an imprint of Houghton Mifflin Harcourt Publishing Company.

www.hmhbooks.com

The illustrations were executed in acrylic-gouache.
The text was set in 16-pt. Weiss Roman.
Hand-lettering by Leah Palmer Preiss

LIBRARY OF CONGRESS CATALOGING-IN-PUBLICATION DATA

Park, Linda Sue.
The third gift / by Linda Sue Park ; illustrated by Bagram Ibatoulline.
p. cm.
Summary: After harvesting an especially large "tear" of a resin known as myrrh, a young boy and his father visit a spice merchant whose three customers are seeking a special gift to bring to a baby. Includes biblical references and historical information about the Magi and myrrh.
ISBN 978-0-547-20195-5 (hardcover : alk. paper) [1. Myrrh—Fiction. 2. Fathers and sons—Fiction. 3. Magi—Fiction. 4. Jesus Christ—Nativity—Fiction.] I. Ibatoulline, Bagram, ill. II. Title.
PZ7.P22115Thi 2011
[E]—dc22
2010050819

Manufactured in Singapore
TWP 10 9 8 7 6 5 4 3 2 1
4500306494

To Marjorie Naughton
—L.S.P.

To Maria Brodsky
—B.I.

My father collects tears. That is what they are called: the pearls of sap that seep out of a tree when the bark is cut. Maybe they are called tears because it seems as if the tree is crying.

My father knows where the good trees are. I walk with him, the basket in one hand, the water-gourd slung over my shoulder. We walk a long way.

Some of the trees are close together. But most of them are far apart. One tree here. Another tree there. Yet another far beyond.

They are not beautiful trees. Their branches are stunted, knotty, spiny. Their leaves are a dull grayish green.

My father has to see *inside* each tree.

Of course he can't *really* see inside. But he looks carefully at the trunk, and the branches. He tears off a leaf and sniffs it. He runs his hand along the bark.

Sometimes he shakes his head. *No. Not this tree. Not now.*

And we walk again, in the heat and dust.

Other times, he nods his head and takes up the ax.

This is another thing he knows: how to cut through the bark twice, in the shape of an *X*. Not too deep. Not too shallow. And in exactly the right place.

He makes the first cut, then the second. He steps back. Together, we watch.

I hold my breath.

A tear begins to emerge. A tear of sap, the blood of the tree.

If my father has chosen well—and he always does, for he has been harvesting these tears all his life—plenty of sap will bubble out from a pocket beneath the bark. It will form a fine big tear before the sap ceases flowing.

The outside of the tear will dry in the hot sun, until he can pick it off with his fingers.

My father's tears are large, their rough dried shell protecting the treasure of resin within. Other collectors are not as skilled as he is. Their tears are small, all shell and no center.

My father sells the tears to the spice merchant in the marketplace. Because the tears take time and skill to harvest, they fetch good sums of money—and people must pay even more to buy them.

The tears are used for many things. They can be ground up as medicine for headaches or stomachaches. They are used to flavor wine. Some people like to rub the resin on their skin, to soothe rashes.

The best tears, the most expensive ones, are used for funerals.

The tears are ground into a powder, then steeped in oil. The oil is used to wash the body of the one who has died.

Other tears are burned during the funeral, so their scent fills the air. It is a sharp smell, both bitter and sweet.

When you smell the tears at a funeral, you know that someone truly beloved has died.

My father takes me with him to harvest the tears. He holds out a leaf for me to sniff. He tells me to run my hand over the bark of a tree.

I do not yet know what I am supposed to smell, or feel.

But one day I will. Until then, I carry the basket and the water-gourd. And I watch, and try to learn.

My father checks the last of the good trees. He smiles. "Look," he says.

I look, and see the biggest tear yet. As large as a hen's egg. Nearly as large as my fist!

"Go ahead," he says, still smiling.

I set the basket down and reach for the tear. I twist it off carefully but quickly, just as I have seen him do it. I hold it in my palm, turn it over, sniff its sharp, bitter sweetness.

Then I place it gently in the basket.

On the way home, I look at it again and again.

A few weeks later, we walk to the market. It is after midday when we arrive.

The spice merchant waves and calls to us. "I have been waiting for you!"

Inside his tent, there are three men drinking tea. They wear fine robes—red, gold, blue. I have never seen such robes before.

The spice merchant says to his customers, "This is the man I was telling you about."

The man in red greets my father. "We are buying gifts," he says. "We have some already, but we wish to buy one more. Something special."

My father nods at me. I give the basket to the merchant. With practiced fingers, he culls through the tears and places several of the largest on a cloth.

In the center is *my* tear.

The three men examine the tears. They speak to one another in a strange language. Finally they look at the merchant and my father, and they nod.

"We have a gift of gold, and a gift of frankincense," says the man in red. "Now we will add to them a gift of myrrh."

As the spice merchant wraps the tears, he says, "May I ask who the gifts are for?"

I am glad he asked, for I want to know too.

The man in red does not speak for a moment. Then he says, "The gifts are for a baby."

I frown a little. Myrrh is a strange gift to give to a baby. But of course, I say nothing. And I am proud that my tear, the one I harvested, is to be part of the gift.

I watch the three men mount their camels.
I watch them leave the marketplace.
I watch as they ride into the desert.
And I wonder about the baby.

AUTHOR'S NOTE

Now after Jesus was born in Bethlehem of Judea in the days of Herod the king, behold, wise men from the East came to Jerusalem, saying, "Where is He who has been born King of the Jews? For we have seen His star in the East and have come to worship Him."

—the Gospel according to St. Matthew, chapter 2, verses 1–2

The visit of the Magi to Bethlehem appears in just one place in the Bible, in the second chapter of the book of Matthew, verses 1–12. Indeed, only two of the four Gospels of the New Testament depict the birth of Christ at all. Luke mentions the visit of the shepherds to the stable (2:8–20), but not the Magi, whereas Matthew describes the journey of the Magi but says nothing about the shepherds.

Matthew does not specify the number of wise men. Artists' portrayals of the Magi over the years depict different numbers. Renaissance paintings show as many as a dozen Magi crowded around the Mother and Child. A few hundred years later, Flemish artists such as Peter Paul Rubens and Jan Brueghel the Elder painted three Magi in their Nativity scenes—perhaps because Matthew mentions three gifts in his text:

And when they had come into the house, they saw the young Child with Mary His mother, and fell down and worshiped Him. And when they had opened their treasures, they presented gifts to Him: gold, frankincense, and myrrh.

—Matthew 2:11

The belief that there were three wise men is the one that prevails today, its popularity no doubt bolstered for recent generations of Christians by the famous hymn by John H. Hopkins Jr., "We Three Kings of Orient Are" (1857).

In Western Christianity, the Magi are most commonly known by the names Caspar (or Gaspar), Melchior, and Balthazar. These names may have descended from Greek tradition. Several other sects throughout history have used different names, and no one is quite sure who these "three kings" were.

Behold, the star which they had seen in the East went before them, till it came and stood over where the young Child was.

When they saw the star, they rejoiced with exceedingly great joy.

—Matthew 2:9–10

Matthew says that the wise men came from "the East" but gives no other details of their provenance. There are several hypotheses about exactly where in "the East" their trip might have originated.

Because the Magi used a star to guide them, some historians have theorized that they may have been Zoroastrian priests. Named for the prophet Zoroaster, the religion was established centuries before Christ's birth, and its priests were famed for their expertise in astronomy. Zoroastrianism was practiced most widely in the area then known as Persia (now the country of Iran). It spread across the Middle East, and today the largest Zoroastrian communities are in India.

Whether the Magi came from Persia or farther afield, they might have traveled to Bethlehem through the Arabian Peninsula. The peninsula and the area directly across the Red Sea from it (Ethiopia and Somalia today) were major centers for the production of myrrh.

Myrrh is the name used for several plants of the *Commiphora* genus. These small trees or shrubs are native to the Arabian Peninsula in what is now Yemen, as well as parts of northeastern Africa. The name *myrrh* is also ascribed to another plant found on the Indian subcontinent (*Balsamodendron myrrha*).

Myrrh has been valued throughout history in many parts of the world. The Persian, Egyptian, Roman, Chinese, and Indian cultures all treasured myrrh. It was used in incense, perfume, and embalming oil, as an additive to wine, and as a medicinal herb.

This story came about because as a child, when I heard the Nativity story over and over, I never knew what "myrrh" was. Nobody else ever asked, so I thought everyone knew but me. Not until I was an adult did I find out what myrrh is, and that in ancient times it was primarily used as an embalming oil and funerary incense.

After I completed the manuscript of this story, I learned that the narrator and I are not the only ones to have wondered about a baby gift so imbued with connotations of death. In 1564, the artist Pieter Brueghel the Elder seems to have had similar thoughts. His painting *The Adoration of the Kings*, which hangs in the National Gallery in London, shows the infant Jesus on his mother's lap, surrounded by the Magi and other onlookers. One of the Magi is presenting a gift to the Child, and the curator's label reads in part: "The tiny, naked Christ Child . . . recoils from the gift of myrrh, the spice used to prepare bodies for burial, foreseeing in it his future death."

As for the young narrator himself, I love thinking about the roles of ordinary people in history's great events. History is happening all around us every day, and stories can help remind us that we are as much a part of it as those whose names dominate the headlines.